Word List

Here is a list of words that might make it easier to read this book. You'll find them in boldface the first time they appear in the story.

commander	kuh-MAN-der
specialist	SPE-shuh-list
simulator	SIM-yuh-lay-ter
astronauts	AS-truh-nauts
telescope	TE-luh-skohp
robotic	roh-BO-tik
astronomer	uh-STRO-nuh-mer
galaxy	GA-lek-see
mechanism	ME-kuh-ni-zum
sensitive	SEN-suh-tiv
gravity	GRA-vuh-tee
insulated	IN-suh-layt-id
oxygen	OK-si-jen
deafening	DE-fuh-ning
satellite	SA-tuhl-eyt
atmosphere	AT-muh-sfear

Shooting for the Stars

BARBIE and associated trademarks are owned by and used under license from Mattel, Inc. © 1998 Mattel, Inc. All Rights Reserved. Published by Grolier Books, a division of Grolier Enterprises, Inc. Story by Karen Stillman and Victoria Saxon. Photo crew: Hervé Grison, Mary Hirahara, Susan Cracraft, Patrick Kittel, Robert Guillaume, and Lisa Collins. Produced by Bumpy Slide Books. Printed in the United States of America.

ISBN: 0-7172-8830-7

GROLIER
B O O K S

Chapter One

"Launch minus nine minutes," said the voice over Barbie's headset.

Barbie checked the control panel in the cockpit of the shuttle. As the mission's pilot, she had a seat in the front of the space shuttle. Next to her sat the mission **commander,** David. Behind Barbie sat Kira, the mission **specialist** and a good friend of Barbie's. Kira was trained to do special experiments up in space.

Barbie strained to hear the voice from mission control. But the voice was getting weaker and harder to understand. Suddenly she couldn't hear anything at all.

Barbie glanced at David. He looked worried.

Barbie knew that if she could not hear the engineers at the control station outside the shuttle, then they probably could not hear her. Still, she had to try. "Mission control," she said, "we have lost contact with you."

There was no response. Barbie tried to stay calm. She knew that without contact with the engineers at mission control, it would be up to her to make sure it was safe to launch the shuttle. Barbie paused. Once, long ago, she had learned that the best way to make important decisions was to stay calm and think clearly. She knew she should do that right now.

Barbie thought about the steps of a successful launch. Then she checked the time. Now only eight minutes remained to launch time. That meant that the walkway the crew used to get onto the shuttle should be pulling away. But when Barbie looked out her window, she saw that it was still in place. Something was wrong.

Barbie took a deep breath. She did not want to cancel the launch without a good reason. But if the walkway wasn't removed in time, the shuttle could rip it apart during the launch. Barbie reached for the control panel. She pushed the alarm button.

Instantly, flashing red lights filled the cockpit.

David looked at Barbie and nodded, giving her a "thumbs-up" sign. She had done the right thing by sounding the alarm!

"That was pretty exciting for an indoor liftoff," David joked as soon as Barbie and Kira had taken off their headsets.

They all sighed. It was true. The experience had felt real, even though they had been in a **simulator** the whole time. The shuttle simulator at the Texas space center was used to train **astronauts.** It looked and felt like a space shuttle, but it never actually left the ground.

"What happened?" Kira asked. "I heard there were nine minutes until launch, and then suddenly everything went silent."

"I'm not sure," Barbie replied. "But I think it may have had something to do with the walkway not moving away from the shuttle."

"I think you're right, Barbie," David said. "Let's go out and see."

Barbie felt great. This had only been a test. If she did all the right things, then she might finally be able to go into space. But if she made a mistake, it might be months or even years before she would get to go.

David was the first one to step out through the hatch of the shuttle simulator. Barbie and Kira climbed out behind him.

Dr. Carol Foster, the director of the space training center, stood outside waiting for them. She was the one who would decide who would fly into space. She took her job very seriously.

"I just watched your simulation," Dr. Foster announced as soon as she saw the three astronauts. "And I want to say that you all did excellent work."

Barbie breathed a sigh of relief. Then Dr. Foster continued, "I'm going to be holding a meeting with a select group of astronauts in about an hour. I'd like the three of you to attend."

"We'll be there!" David declared.

After the friends changed out of their space suits, they went to the meeting room. Dr. Foster stood at the front of the room and welcomed the astronauts.

"Thank you for coming today," she began. "As you all know, a few years ago we put a **telescope** called the Mitchell into space. Now we can see planets and stars we never knew were there."

Dr. Foster cleared her throat. "But we have a problem," she said. "The latest pictures from the

Mitchell Telescope are not clear. Something inside it is not working correctly. We need a team to go up and fix it. We have chosen five of our best astronauts to be on that team."

Barbie and Kira leaned forward in their chairs. They were very excited. They had dreamed about a chance like this. Everyone in the room wondered who the lucky astronauts would be.

Chapter Two

"First we need some crew members who have been in space before," said Dr. Foster. "I'm choosing David to be the mission commander. David has flown on three space missions."

Barbie glanced at David and smiled. She could tell that he was excited.

"One of our mission specialists will be Dan," said Dr. Foster.

A man with light brown hair and a mustache stood up. Barbie knew Dan. He had flown on the space shuttle before.

"The third member of the crew will operate

the **robotic** arm," Dr. Foster explained. "Robin operated it on our last mission to space. She will be joining the crew this time as well."

Robin stood up. She had short, red hair and green eyes.

Kira sighed. "There's no hope for us now," she whispered to Barbie. "Each of these crew members has flown at least one mission. They have all been astronauts for years!"

Barbie crossed her fingers. Maybe Kira was right. Maybe they had no chance of being chosen. But it didn't hurt to hope.

"The last two crew members will be newcomers," said Dr. Foster. "But I think you will all agree with me that they are ready for the challenge."

Dr. Foster smiled at Kira and Barbie. "Barbie will be the shuttle pilot, and Kira will be the mission specialist in charge of fixing the telescope."

Kira almost jumped out of her seat. Barbie's eyes opened wide. They couldn't believe it! They were really going on a space mission. And they were going together!

As David and Dan leaned over to congratulate the two friends, Dr. Foster continued. "The rest of the people in this room will be part of the ground crew. They will help the astronauts through their mission. Congratulations to all of you!"

Everyone applauded.

"Now let me explain what the Mitchell's problem is and how we need you to fix it," Dr. Foster began.

Dr. Foster showed the group a large drawing of the telescope. "This is the Mitchell Telescope. It is named after Maria Mitchell, America's first woman **astronomer.** The Mitchell can see farther and more clearly than any telescope on Earth," she explained.

"It's simply amazing!" said Kira.

"Yes, it's quite wonderful," Dr. Foster agreed. "The Mitchell has a special camera that sends pictures back to Earth. But now the pictures are blurry, and important information is being lost."

"That's why it has to be fixed," said Barbie. "We could be learning so much more about our **galaxy**!"

"That's right," said Dr. Foster.

"How exactly is the mission going to work?" asked Robin.

Dr. Foster pointed to the picture of the Mitchell. "Barbie will steer the shuttle close enough to the Mitchell so that repairs can be made safely and quickly. Robin will be in charge of grasping the Mitchell with the shuttle's robotic arm. Kira and Dan will actually go out into space and adjust the focusing **mechanism.** As mission commander, David will be in charge of making sure that the job runs smoothly overall."

Dr. Foster talked more about the details of

the mission. She also explained how the engineers at mission control would help. When she finished, the group thanked her and left the room.

"Wow," Barbie said as they walked down the hallway. "We have a lot to learn in the next few months."

"That's right," David agreed. "Training will be hard. But once we're in space, we'll be glad we did our homework."

The next day, the five astronauts met in a small meeting room. They were waiting for their trainer to arrive. Suddenly the door swung open, and a small woman with curly brown hair strode in.

David groaned quietly as soon as he saw her. "That's Caroline Shreds. I've worked with her before," he whispered to Barbie. "She's good, but she's tough. They call her the 'Shredder'."

"Good morning," said Caroline. "I believe you all know me. I'll be in charge of your training for the mission. Now, before we start, I should tell you I only have one motto."

Everyone leaned forward.

"Practice! Practice! Practice!" Caroline stated. "You are going to practice until you can do your jobs standing on your heads!"

Robin laughed. "And in space, we may have to!" she whispered to Kira.

As soon as the training began, the team spent a lot more time in the shuttle simulator. They needed to become comfortable working together in a small space.

Then the astronauts began to focus on their special tasks. David learned everything about the shuttle. Robin spent many hours working with the robotic arm. Barbie practiced flying and landing. She also practiced steering the shuttle the way she would in space. And Kira learned everything she could about the Mitchell Telescope and how to focus it.

"Your job won't be easy," Caroline said to

Kira. "You won't have much time to fix the problem. And some parts of the Mitchell are very **sensitive.** One bump could damage the entire telescope."

"That would be awful," said Barbie.

"Yes," agreed Caroline. "That's why my motto is so important."

"Practice, practice, practice!" said Barbie and Kira at the same time. They laughed. Then they started practicing all over again.

Chapter Three

One night, after a hard day of training, the astronauts walked to their cars together. It was a clear night, and the stars were shining brightly.

"I always wanted to fly in space," confessed Robin as she gazed up at the night sky. "Ever since I can remember, I used to look up at the stars and wonder what it would be like to visit them."

Barbie smiled at Robin. It was nice to know someone else felt the same way she did.

"I used to build space rockets as a kid," said Dan. "But I never thought I would ride in one!"

"I was good at math," David said. Then he

added with a smile, "And when I realized that math skills were an important part of becoming an astronaut, I knew what I wanted to do."

"Me, too!" cried Kira. "I always loved math and science. But it was my third-grade teacher who first suggested I use them in space."

Then David turned to Barbie. "What made you interested in becoming an astronaut?" he asked.

"Ever since I was a little girl, I have loved looking at the stars," Barbie said quietly. "For my tenth birthday, I got my first real telescope. During the summer, my favorite thing was to sit out on the deck at night and look at the stars."

Kira spoke up. "You know, Barbie, you sound just like the astronomer Maria Mitchell as a girl."

David laughed. "How perfect that this is your first mission."

Everyone was quiet for a moment.

Barbie smiled. "I still have that telescope. It's hard to believe that we'll soon be up there with the stars."

Everyone agreed. Then they said their goodnights and got into their cars.

The next day, Barbie's and Kira's friend Ken came to visit them at the space center.

"How's training going?" Ken asked.

"It's hard work, but we're learning a lot," answered Barbie.

"Tomorrow we're going swimming!" Kira added.

Ken looked confused. "Wait a minute," he said. "Is this a space center or a sleep-away camp?"

Kira and Barbie laughed.

"Water is the one place on Earth where people float as they do in space, without **gravity**," explained Barbie.

"So we're going to practice the whole thing in a big pool," said Kira.

"Sounds like fun. But aren't you two nervous?" asked Ken.

"A little," Barbie admitted. "There is a lot to remember."

"I'm sure you'll do fine. You have both been working so hard," said Ken. "And if you decide you don't like being astronauts, you can always work as lifeguards!"

Early the next morning, the shuttle crew reported to a special pool. In the pool were a model of the Mitchell and model parts of the shuttle.

All the astronauts dressed for the practice mission. They had to wear many layers of special clothing. Each space suit had different markings on the sides. These markings helped the astronauts tell each other apart when they were in their suits.

Before going into the water, the team put on heavy boots and **insulated** gloves that would keep them warm in space. They also put on **oxygen** tanks. The oxygen tanks would help the crew breathe during their underwater training. Later the tanks would help the astronauts get enough oxygen to breathe in space.

Under their helmets, the astronauts wore soft caps with built-in microphones. The microphones would help the astronauts speak with their trainers while they were underwater. Once they got into space, they would use the microphones to speak to mission control on Earth.

"Can you imagine doing this every morning?" Barbie said through her microphone.

"By the time we would finish getting dressed, it would be time to get into pajamas!" Kira joked.

When all the astronauts were in their suits, they were lowered into the water with a crane. They practiced the planned mission from the beginning.

Soon it was time for Kira to begin her work on the Mitchell. Dan tried to hold the bulky equipment steady while Kira removed the covering on the telescope.

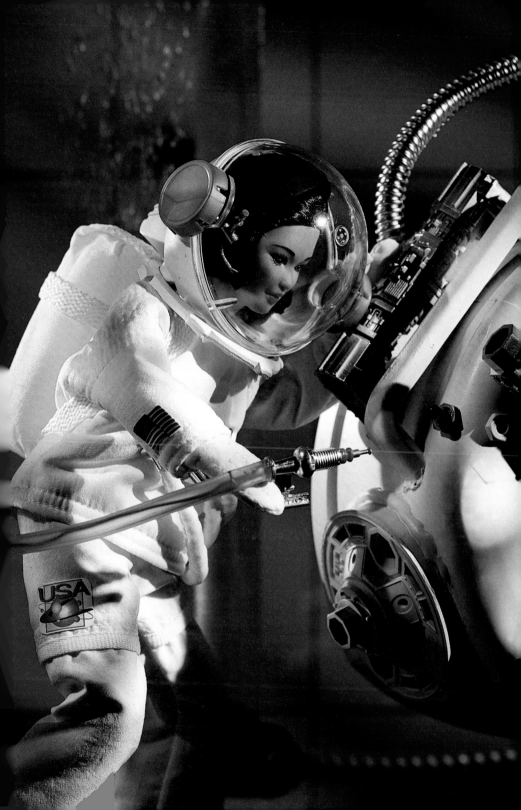

"So far, so good," Barbie said as she watched.

Suddenly one of the tools bumped into the camera on the telescope.

"Oh, no!" Kira exclaimed. She knew that she could not have such an accident in space. It could delay their mission and ruin their hopes of fixing the telescope.

After practice, Caroline approached Kira and Barbie. "We're going to try that same exercise tomorrow, Kira," Caroline said. "We need to do it over and over until you get it right."

As Caroline walked away, Barbie turned toward Kira.

"Don't worry, Kira," Barbie said to her friend. "That's why we practice so much."

Kira nodded. "I know you're right, Barbie," she said. "I just hope I don't make the same mistake tomorrow."

Chapter Four

Before Barbie knew it, two months had passed. Caroline had worked with all the astronauts, helping them practice their jobs until they performed them over and over with no mistakes.

Soon the whole crew flew to the space center in Florida. Everyone went to sleep early the night before the launch. They would have to wake up very early to be ready by 7:30 A.M.

At three o'clock in the morning, Barbie felt someone gently shake her. It was Kira.

"I can't believe this day has finally arrived," Kira said excitedly.

Barbie stretched and got out of bed. After she had dressed, she reached into her bag and pulled out a pocket-size tool kit.

"What's that?" asked Kira.

"It's the kit of tools that came with my first telescope," Barbie replied. "I wanted to bring it as a good-luck charm."

"I understand," said Kira. "I'm wearing a watch my sister gave me. It will help remind me of my family when I'm so far from home."

The two friends hugged each other quickly and then went out into the crisp early morning air. They headed toward the van that would take them to the launchpad. They could see the other astronauts already there. Barbie and Kira also saw reporters, friends, and family members waiting to wave good-bye.

"Look, there's Ken!" said Kira.

Cameras flashed. The reporters called out questions. Barbie was glad to see Ken's friendly face among the strangers.

"Are you excited?" one reporter yelled out to Barbie.

"I've never been more excited in my life!" Barbie replied.

"Are you nervous?" asked another reporter.

"I've never been more *nervous* in my life," Barbie said with a laugh.

Barbie turned and waved to Ken, then headed toward the other astronauts.

"Just a minute," said a voice. It was Dr. Foster. Barbie could tell from Dr. Foster's face that something was wrong.

"I just got the weather report," said Dr. Foster. "It's too windy to blast off now. Let's see if the wind dies down in the next few hours. If it doesn't, we may have to delay the mission."

Barbie sighed. She had waited so long to go into space. She didn't want to wait anymore! But she also knew they couldn't blast off if it was too windy. As the pilot, Barbie knew that if anything went wrong with the launch, they would have to return to the ground. Even for the most experienced pilots, windy weather could be dangerous.

Barbie waited with the other astronauts in a building near the launchpad.

"I hope we don't have to wait until tomorrow," said Kira. "I'm nervous enough as it is."

Finally Dr. Foster came in. "Well," she said, "I've got some news."

The astronauts held their breath. "The winds have died down," said Dr. Foster. "The shuttle will go up today as planned!"

Everyone cheered. Then they headed toward the shuttle. When the astronauts arrived at the launchpad, they rode a special elevator up to the top of a tower next to the shuttle. As Barbie stepped out of the elevator and strode across the walkway, she remembered the simulator test she had taken several months earlier. She had come a

long way since then.

All the members of the crew entered the shuttle through a hatch. Then they took their positions inside.

After Barbie had settled into her seat, she looked out her window and gazed at the Atlantic Ocean. "It sure is beautiful out there," she said.

"I'll take your word for it," Dan said with a laugh. "We can't see a thing back here!"

It was true. As the pilot and mission commander, only Barbie and David had views.

Since it was a long wait until launch, Barbie and the other astronauts reviewed their notes. Then they began making sure everything in the shuttle was fastened down. Otherwise, they would find all sorts of things floating in the cabin when the shuttle reached space!

Soon mission control told the shuttle crew that blastoff was only minutes away. Then the astronauts heard a familiar voice. It was Caroline

She was speaking to them from mission control.

"I just want all of you to know that practice makes perfect, and you all have practiced enough to do a great job," Caroline said. "Good luck! I'll be in voice contact with you the whole way."

Then the countdown began. "Ten . . . nine . . . eight . . . "

Barbie looked at the control panel in front of her. Everything was in order.

"Five . . . four . . . three . . . " came the voice from mission control. The shuttle was shaking now. Barbie could hear the roar of the engines outside.

"Two . . . one . . . Blastoff!"

Barbie held on tightly to the edge of her seat. She didn't need to steer the shuttle yet. The noise of the blasting rockets was **deafening.** As the shuttle lurched upward, the astronauts were pressed back into their seats.

In a few minutes, Barbie caught a glimpse of the rocket boosters ripping away from the shuttle.

The rockets spun away and drifted toward the ocean below as the shuttle sailed into space.

Suddenly the shuttle stopped shaking. Everything was silent. The sky outside Barbie's window was dark. Barbie closed her eyes. She wanted to be able to remember this feeling forever.

She was finally in space!

Chapter Five

Looking out the window, Barbie saw the Earth. How beautiful it was! There were some white clouds, some spots of green and brown where there was land, and lots and lots of blue water.

"From here, you can really see how much of the Earth is water," David pointed out.

"Well, from here, you can't see much at all!" joked Kira. She was straining to look outside from her seat in the back of the shuttle.

The crew laughed. The mission was off to a good start. It would take three days to reach the

Mitchell Telescope. So far they were right on schedule. Everyone was in great spirits.

Now that they were in space, the astronauts could get out of their seats and take off their bulky space suits. They no longer needed them for protection. They were much more comfortable wearing T-shirts and pants.

Barbie soon found herself floating up to the ceiling. She could even do a somersault in the air!

Then they saw their first sunset in space. It was beautiful. When the light faded, the astronauts could even make out the twinkling of city lights on the face of the darkened Earth.

When it was time to go to bed, the astronauts pulled out their sleeping bags. The sleeping bags had special back supports. Some of the astronauts also wore eyeshades to keep out any light.

Because there was no gravity pulling them down, the crew could sleep anywhere in the shuttle. Barbie attached her sleeping bag to one of the walls. Robin chose to float around as if she were a person rising in a magic trick.

"I think I'll sleep upside down on the ceiling," said Kira. "When I was little, my mom painted flowers on the ceiling of my room. I always wished I could crawl up and sleep in my flower garden."

"Maybe you'll dream about flowers," said Barbie.

"Most of my dreams these days are about telescopes," replied Kira.

Everyone smiled, said goodnight, and went to sleep.

About five hours later, it was time to start a new day in space.

"Well," said Barbie, "how about something to eat?" She and Dan offered to make breakfast for the crew.

For their first breakfast in space, the crew decided on eggs and fruit. Barbie added water

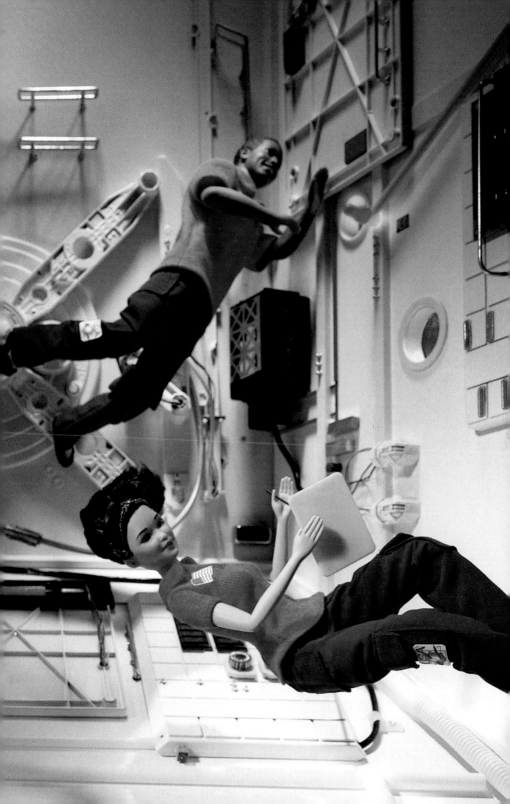

to packages of scrambled eggs that had already been cooked and freeze-dried. She put the packages in a special oven.

The astronauts' food had to be secured to food trays.

When the crew tried to eat their eggs, they had to scoop them out carefully with their spoons. Otherwise the eggs, too, would float freely around the cabin.

David liked to be right-side up when he ate, so he attached himself to a wall. Kira decided to dine upside down, on the ceiling. Barbie floated as she ate.

"I remember when astronauts first began going to outer space," David said. "They had to eat goop from a tube."

"We're lucky. Food has gotten a lot better!" said Robin. She gently tossed an apple in David's direction. He pushed away from the wall with his foot and caught the apple in his mouth.

"Maybe this food's better," said Dan, "but when I get back to Earth, I'm going to eat a big, juicy hamburger."

"And french fries," added Robin.

Suddenly Kira cried out, "Oh, no! There goes my apple juice!" It had escaped from its container. Now it formed into the shape of a ball and floated around the inside of the cabin.

"Try to catch it!" cried David. He gently pushed Kira in the direction of her juice. When she had floated close enough, she carefully stabbed the little golden ball with her straw. Then she began drinking the juice through the straw as the others watched and laughed.

The astronauts spent the next two days conducting tests. The tests would give scientists on Earth more information about space. By the third day, they were ready to repair the Mitchell.

"We should be able to spot the telescope any time now," said David.

Barbie turned and looked outside. There in the blackness, she saw the Mitchell Telescope. "I think our wait is over," she said. "There it is right now."

"Great!" said David. "Barbie, do your stuff!"

Barbie carefully steered the shuttle until it was close to the Mitchell.

Meanwhile, Robin had begun to work the controls on the robotic arm. She pressed the buttons skillfully. It was important for the arm to grab the telescope on the first try. If it missed, the Mitchell could drift out of reach before the team had another chance.

Barbie concentrated on keeping the shuttle steady. She wanted to make Robin's job as easy as possible.

"I've got it!" Robin cried.

"Hooray!" said Kira.

"Nice job," added Barbie.

David radioed Caroline at mission control.

He told her the first stage of the mission was a success. Through her headset, Barbie heard Caroline and everyone at mission control cheer.

"Okay," David said, turning to Dan and Kira. "It's time for you two to take a walk in space!"

Chapter Six

David and Robin helped Dan and Kira put on their space suits. Then Dan and Kira went into a special airlock area with Robin. The airlock area helped keep the shuttle's air supply from escaping when the astronauts went outside.

"Good luck!" Barbie called from the cockpit.

"Thanks," said Kira. "I hope I don't bump into anything."

"Don't worry," said Barbie. "It looks like a slow traffic day in space."

Robin helped Kira and Dan put on their helmets. Then she returned to the cabin and closed the door.

Minutes later, the two astronauts were ready to step into space. When the door opened, they stepped out together into blackness.

For a moment, they just floated there. It was very quiet. They looked at the endless numbers of stars all around them.

"Are you okay?" asked Barbie from the cockpit.

"Yes," Kira said. "It's beautiful out here."

Barbie carefully monitored the shuttle's movements while Dan and Kira checked the cables that attached them to the shuttle.

Then they slowly made their way through the darkness toward the Mitchell. Once there, Dan held onto the giant telescope while Kira gently removed part of the Mitchell's casing. Then Kira looked inside.

Carefully, Kira reached for one of the tools that was attached to her space suit and set to work.

A couple of hours later, the work on the Mitchell was still going smoothly. Barbie had just checked in with Dan when she heard Kira say "Oh, no!"

"What's wrong?" Barbie asked.

"I don't have the right size screwdriver," Kira said. "The ones I have are all too big."

"Did you have it with you earlier?" David asked.

"Yes," Kira replied. "I know I did. I don't know what could have happened to it."

"Don't worry," David told her. "We'll try to find it in here. Maybe it floated behind something in the cabin. For now, I want you two to come back inside."

While Barbie stayed in the cockpit, the other members of the crew helped Dan and Kira back onboard the shuttle. Then they began searching the cabin for the lost screwdriver. But it was nowhere to be found.

David reported the bad news to Barbie.

Suddenly Barbie had an idea. "Kira," she asked, "does it have to be the screwdriver from your kit?"

Kira thought for a moment. "I don't think so," she replied. "I just need something that's the right size to turn the screw."

Barbie smiled. "I think I have just what you need."

Barbie pulled out a screwdriver from her old telescope tool kit. She could tell by the look on Kira's face that the tool's size looked just right.

David told mission control what had happened.

Caroline was worried. "We don't know if this new tool will work," she said. "I'd rather not take the risk of damaging the telescope. Everything should be tested on the ground first."

Barbie spoke up. "Caroline, I know this is a hard decision to make," she said. "But isn't it better if we try with what we have rather than give up now? If we work carefully, we still have a good chance of fixing the telescope."

For a minute or two, no one spoke. Then the shuttle crew heard Caroline's voice again. "Okay," she said. "But be careful. And remember, you know exactly what to do. This is just like another practice session."

"A-l-l right!" shouted Dan. He was so happy that he performed a back flip in the air! The other astronauts watched and laughed. They were all excited!

It took a few hours for the crew to get ready. They went through the same steps they had done earlier to prepare Kira and Dan for their mission. Robin helped Kira attach the new screwdriver to her space suit. When they were ready, Kira and Dan floated outside once again.

Barbie held the shuttle steady while Kira and Dan worked. The other astronauts waited inside the shuttle. They were ready to act in case something went wrong. Back on Earth, Caroline and the rest of the ground crew waited anxiously.

Kira was working slowly and carefully.

"You can do it, Kira," Barbie said to her through their headsets. "Just take your time."

Finally they heard a little gasp from Kira.

"What is it?" David asked. "Is everything okay, Kira?"

Kira laughed. "It's better than okay. It's great!" she cried. "We did it!"

"Whew!" said Barbie. "That was close!"

Once the two astronauts were safely back inside the ship, David said, "Nice going, Kira and Dan! You saved the Mitchell!"

"Thanks," said Kira. "But we couldn't have done it without Barbie's screwdriver."

As Barbie started preparing for their return home, she noticed a warning on her control screen. Mission control was telling her to watch for something outside. "Oh, my!" she exclaimed.

"What is it?" Kira asked.

"It looks like part of an old **satellite,**" David answered. "As you know, lots of satellite pieces break off and float around space like that. The only problem is that this chunk of 'space trash' seems to be headed straight toward the Mitchell!"

"What should we do?" Dan asked calmly.

"Robin, can the robotic arm hold onto the Mitchell while the shuttle is moving?" David asked.

"Maybe," Robin replied. "What are you thinking?"

"I'm thinking that if you can hold onto the Mitchell, then Barbie can move the shuttle," he explained. "And we'll drag the Mitchell to safety."

"Great idea," said Robin. "But you'll have to be careful. If the shuttle moves too fast, we might lose our grip on the telescope."

Barbie looked at the object floating toward the Mitchell. Then she began to move the shuttle.

She had to move at just the right speed to keep a grip on the Mitchell and get out of the way of the trash. The space trash floated closer and closer. But Barbie gently guided the shuttle as it dragged the telescope through space.

"Great work, Barbie!" David exclaimed as the trash sailed safely past their window.

"Whew! Thanks," Barbie replied. "Thanks to you, too. That was a good idea! Okay, Robin, you can release the Mitchell now."

"Congratulations to all of you," said David. "Now let's turn this ship around and go home!"

"Is everything secure?" David asked the crew. He was reading from a checklist. "We still have a few things to do before returning to Earth. Are the tools packed away? Are the airlock doors shut?"

The entire crew checked twice to make sure everything was in its proper place.

"Everything looks good," David said to Barbie. "Let's head for home."

Barbie started to pilot the shuttle on its trip back to Earth. The shuttle had been moving very fast in space. To land on Earth, it needed to slow down. To do this, Barbie turned the shuttle in the opposite direction for a while.

"It feels like riding backward on a train!" exclaimed Kira.

Now Barbie turned the shuttle back around. It was flying nose-first again.

"We've slowed to 24,356 feet per second," Barbie reported.

"Look!" David called. He pointed out the window to the tiles on the shuttle's surface. "The tiles are glowing red-hot. We must be entering Earth's **atmosphere.**"

"I always love that color," said Robin. "That glow on the tiles means we're almost home."

"Yes," said Dan. "Good old Planet Earth!"

"All right," said Barbie a while later. "We're preparing to land."

She could see the runway up ahead in the middle of a desert. But her job was far from over. She worked quickly with David to guide the shuttle toward the runway. The shuttle was still traveling at more than 200 miles per hour. Barbie took a deep breath. She lowered the wheels just minutes before the shuttle was to touch down on land.

"Main landing gear touchdown," Barbie said as the back wheels of the shuttle eased onto the runway. Then the front wheel came down with a bump. "Nosegear touchdown."

Slowly the shuttle glided to a complete stop. Barbie was so excited. She had just completed her first *real* shuttle landing!

Barbie heard Caroline's voice through her headset. "Welcome home, everyone!" Caroline said. "Perfect landing, Barbie and David!"

As the crew left the shuttle, reporters and photographers waited. Cameras clicked, and the newspeople shouted out questions. Everyone was waiting to hear about the mission.

Soon pictures of all the astronauts appeared

in newspapers around the world. And several stories told how the shuttle crew had saved the Mitchell by thinking quickly.

A few weeks later, Barbie got a phone call from Dan. He was arranging for the crew to get together for dinner. They were going to a place that served big, juicy hamburgers and french fries!

It was a clear evening, so they ate outside. Barbie looked up at the stars. "Sometimes I can't believe I was up there," she said. "It was a dream come true."

Everyone agreed. Over dinner they laughed and joked about training with the "Shredder." And then they talked about upcoming missions and their hopes of returning to space.

One week later, Barbie paid a special visit to her old elementary school. The children were delighted that she was there. They had seen her on television and heard their parents talk about the shuttle crew.

Barbie walked onto the stage of the auditorium carrying a large box. She opened it and took out the telescope she had been given for her tenth birthday.

"I want all of you to have this," she told the students in the audience. "Now you can see the wonders of space up close, too." The children were overjoyed.

Later a few of the students came up on stage. Barbie showed them how to look through the telescope and adjust the focus.

"And remember," she added, "when you look up at the stars, don't be afraid to dream."